BE STILL
LITTLE TREE
BE STILL

Shawn Russell
www.bestilltree.com
serpublishing@gmail.com
561-706-8043

Illustrations and Cover Design by: Shawn Elliot Russell

Be Still, Little Tree, Be Still

ISBN-13: 978-0-9972690-7-9 (Paperback)

To my brave little trees,

You are stronger and more amazing
than you could ever know. You are
wonderful and magnificent just the way
you are; a unique and precious gift to
the world. Love yourself with all of
your heart and your life will become
filled with magic and joy. Be still.
I believe in you, you can do it!

Love,

In front of a house
  made of red colored brick,
A yard full of flowers
  and grass that was thick
Was home to a new
  little tree that was planted
Right next to an older tree,
  bigger and *slanted*.

"Hi, Mr. Tree!"
said the new little one.

"Hello there, little tree,
where are you from?"

"I came from a nursery,
it was indoors.
But, I'm loving it here,
there's sunshine galore!"

He was playful and free
with a heart full of glee,
So grateful to be
in that yard by the tree.

Then, one day
the little tree
noticed a change.
The sky became
darker, the clouds
were all strange.
"What's wrong
with the sky,
why does it flash?
What is that grumble?"
the little one asked.

"I almost forgot, you grew up indoors.
Well, little tree, this here is a storm."

BOOM

went the thunder, like dynamite blasts!
It scared little tree, his heart beating fast.
When he got wet, he asked Mr. Tree,
"What is this water that's falling on me?
There's so much I feel like I'm drowning!" he cried.
"That's rain, little friend," the big tree replied.

The little tree shook
  as the gusts of wind blew
    And pushed all his branches,
    pulling them too.
    "I want to go hide,
    I'm scared of the sound.
    I wish I could jump up
     out of the ground
     And run in the house,
     I feel so afraid.
     Oh Please, Mr. Tree,
     make them go away!"

He thought he would help him hide from the storm.
But, Mr. Tree stood there in powerful form
And whispered, not sounding worried or thrilled,

"Be Still, Little Tree, Be Still."

Soon, the clouds
had all passed and
thunder was gone.
The birds all returned
for a feast on the lawn.
The little tree stood there,
soaked from the rain,
Glad it was over
but feeling ashamed.
"I never want to get rained on again.
I hate thunderstorms!"
he said to his friend.
He thought they were bad
'cause they made him afraid.
And, if he stayed away
he'd be safe and okay.

But,
a week
or two later
another one came
And poor little tree
was stuck in the rain.
He'd cry and he'd fight,
shaking in fear,
Praying the lightning
and rain disappeared.
That's when his buddy
would tell him so dear,
"Be Still, Little Tree,
Be Still."

After the storm, the little tree slept;
Tired from all of the tears that he wept.
And when he awoke,
he asked Mr. Tree,
"How come you never
have tried to
help me?

The thunder is scary, the wind tries to push me.
But, you only stand there trying to shush me."

"My dear
little friend,
I do want to help.
That's why
I tell you
what I tell myself.
I once was a tree
even smaller
than you.

And,
one day the storm
came thundering too.
I was afraid
but the tree by the roof said,
"Be Still, Little Tree, Be Still."

She told me that fear
is just like a storm:
It comes out of nowhere
and thunders and pours.

But, sooner or later,
it all goes away.
So, if you are still
then you'll be okay.

Don't run from the storm,
don't fight it or try.
Be still and just feel it
as it passes by.

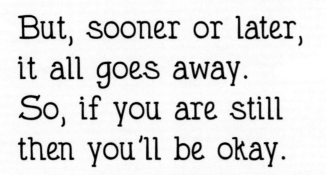

FEEL
the rain
as it falls,
don't say that it's bad.
Hear the roar
of the thunder
that sounds like it's mad.

BE STILL
in the storm,
no matter how strong.

And, before you will know it,
THE STORM WILL BE GONE."

"Is that why you always look
peaceful and calm?"
The little tree asked
as he followed along.
"I still feel afraid,
every now and again,"
Said Mr. Tree to
his curious friend.
"But, when I'm afraid
I say to myself,
'Be still, little tree,
be still' and it helps."

Just as his friend had finished his sentence,
Crashes of lightning struck in the distance.
"Remember, my friend, just try to be still.
The storm may be strong,
but so is your will.
And, if the storm's throwing you
roughly about,
Concentrate on your breath
as it goes in and out."

With that advice, the little tree readied
To follow the steps so he could be steady.
The sky became darker, the storm was now close;
Large and ferocious, stronger than most.

He stood very still,
feeling the winds
Shake all of his branches
and pass through
his limbs.
He stood very still,
and slowly he breathed,
While feeling the rain
pour down
on his leaves.
He stood very still,
hearing the thunder,
Even when wanting
to run under cover.

And, as the wind grew and pushed him around,
He swayed with the wind
while holding his ground.
He said to himself,
under thousands
of drops,

"It's raining right now,
but soon it will stop."
In thunder and lightning,
he peacefully thought,

AFTER AN HOUR,
the storm went away.

It may have been scary, but he was okay.
"Mr. Tree, Mr. Tree, did you see how I did?
I stood really still, and never once hid!"
"I saw, little friend, you made me so proud.
And, now you can make it
through any
grey cloud."
Storms
would arise,
and storms
would depart,
But little
tree always
had peace
in his heart.

Then one day he noticed,
while looking around,
The ground seemed
like it was
a lot further
down.

His trunk had got thicker,
his branches were longer.
He felt kind of different,
bigger, and stronger.
"Hey, Mr. Tree, what's happened to me?
I used to have two branches,
now I have three!"

"The rain,
little tree, it's
helped you get strong.
Sometimes, what we
fear is what helps
us along.
The rain is a gift
that's feeding
your roots.

That's how we grow
leaves and branches
of fruit.
If rain didn't pour,
we'd always be small.
You may think it's bad,
but it's not bad at all."

The little tree stood in amazement and thought,
"The storm that I feared would hurt me a lot
Was really just trying to help me to grow."
And so, when the skies would thunder and glow,
He'd smile and say, so peaceful and slow,
"Be Still, Little Tree, Be Still."

Over the years,
he got even stronger;
The little tree wasn't
so little much longer.
Early one morning,
he opened his eyes
To welcome the sun
and was caught by surprise.
Not too far away,
the length of a car,
Was a new little tree
standing there in the yard.

"Hi,
Mr.
Tree!"
said the
small one to him.
"Hello, little tree,"
he replied with a grin.
"I'm happy to meet you,
where are you from?"
"A nursery," said
the small little one.
They spoke through
the morning and
mid-afternoon,
Until they were stopped
by the sound of a
BOOM.

Both of them stared
at the clouds rolling in,
As they covered the sun
and the sky became grim.
"Mr. Tree, Mr. Tree,
what's going on?
Why is it dark and the
wind blowing strong?"
"I almost forgot,
you grew up indoors.
Well, little tree,
this here is a storm."

The new little tree
looked frozen in fear.
Her eyes became wider,
all glossy
with tears.
"There there,
little tree,
don't be so afraid."
"But I am, Mr. Tree, will we be okay?
Should I try to go hide,
oh what should I do?"
Mr. Tree didn't speak
for a moment
or two.

He stared at the storm,
as he thought of the times
He was terribly terrified
wanting to hide.
But, because of his friend
who was helpful and kind,
He could stand in a storm
and be peaceful inside.
Overcome with emotion,
he smiled and cried,
So grateful that he
was a tree and alive.
Looking back at his scared
little friend, he replied,

"Be Still, Little Tree, Be Still."

Thank you for reading

Be Still
Little Tree
Be Still

Please, be kind to each other.
You never know what kind
of storm someone is
going through in their life.

visit www.bestilltree.com
for additional free resources

Made in the USA
Las Vegas, NV
18 April 2022